Also by
Tommy Greenwald

The Perfect Pitch
(The Good Sports League #2)

Game Changer

Rivals

Dinged

THE GOOD SPORTS LEAGUE

#1
THE ULTIMATE GOAL

BY
TOMMY GREENWALD
ILLUSTRATED BY
LESLEY VAMOS

AMULET BOOKS • NEW YORK

The Library of Congress Control Number for the hardcover edition: 2022032821

Paperback ISBN 978-1-4197-6366-3

Text © 2023 Tommy Greenwald
Illustrations © 2023 Lesley Vamos
Book design by Chelsea Hunter

Excerpt from *The Perfect Pitch*:
Text © 2024 Tommy Greenwald
Illustrations © 2024 Lesley Vamos

Published in paperback in 2023 by Amulet Books, an imprint of ABRAMS. Originally published in hardcover by Amulet Books in 2023. All rights reserved.

Printed and bound in U.S.A.
10 9 8 7 6 5 4 3 2 1

Amulet Books are available at special discounts when purchased in quantity for premiums and promotions as well as fundraising or educational use. Special editions can also be created to specification. For details, contact specialsales@abramsbooks.com or the address below.

Amulet Books® is a registered trademark of Harry N. Abrams, Inc.

ABRAMS The Art of Books
195 Broadway, New York, NY 10007
abramsbooks.com

To the teachers who helped me become the
semirespectable soccer player I used to be:
Coach Chacho
Coach Woog
Coach Loeffler
Coach Lea

CHAPTER ONE

ANCHOVIES VS. BUFFALO CHICKENS

For Ben Cutler, the best part of soccer was the goal celebrations.

Every time he scored, Ben would launch into some sort of ridiculous dance, shaking his hips, hopping on one foot, sometimes even breaking out The Worm. Ben's best friend, Jay-Jay Wright, usually joined in too.

Ben and Jay-Jay played in the Pizza League. That was the unofficial name of the West Harbor town recreation league, because every team was named after a pizza topping. Their team was the Anchovies.

Before every game, their coach, Mr. Song, told the team, "Go have fun out there!" And that's exactly what they did. They had fun—win, lose, or tie.

One day the Anchovies were playing the Buffalo Chickens, and it was a very close game.

The clock was winding down in the second half, and the Buffalo Chickens were winning, 4–3. Everyone was incredibly excited, including Lola, Ben's dog, who was wagging her

The Worm

tail. Lola was a very unusual-looking dog, with one brown eye, one blue eye, one yellow front paw, one red front paw, and two black back paws. She was also an unusual-acting dog, who seemed to understand the rules of soccer, and never ran onto the field until the game was over.

But Lola wasn't an unusual dog in one respect: she loved to chase things. She especially loved chasing animals. And she especially, *especially* loved chasing squirrels. Which is why Lola was wagging her tail so happily: she knew the game was almost over and she would be allowed off the leash for a few minutes, tearing all over the place, looking for trouble.

Ben's parents were at the game too, as was his younger sister, Ellie. But since they didn't have any tails to wag, they yelled and screamed and hollered instead.

"C'MON ANCHOVIES!" yelled Ben's mom.

"YOU CAN DO IT!" screamed Ben's dad.

"SCORE A TOUCHDOWN!" hollered Ellie, who had not yet mastered the rules of soccer.

There were two minutes left in the game, and the Buffalo Chickens had the ball. Lola was licking her lips, thinking about the postgame snack. She was sad when Ben's team lost, but food always made her feel better.

Pretty much like Ben himself.

Then there was one minute left. It looked certain that the Anchovies were going to lose.

But wait . . .

Anchovies midfielder Kevin Dawson gets a head on it. Well, he gets a nose on it. He might need an ice pack after the game.

The ball lands at the feet of Jay-Jay Wright . . . he takes off toward the Chickens' goal . . . teammate Ben Cutler is running right next to him, calling for the ball . . . Jay-Jay doesn't hear him, the crowd is roaring . . .

UH-OH!

Jay-Jay loses the ball! It bounces around . . . Buffalo Chickens and Anchovies are fighting for it . . . Ben Cutler comes away with it!

CHAPTER TWO
THE FLYING MAN DANCE

As soon as the ball hit the back of the net, a lot of things happened:

The Anchovies players, coaches, and families went nuts.

The Buffalo Chickens players, coaches, and families went silent.

Lola started looking around for a squirrel to chase.

And Ben and Jay-Jay launched into their most special goal celebration of all: The Flying Man Dance.

ARMS UP

KICK

STOMP

BEND

FLYING MAN DANCE

SWISH

TWIST

FLY!

The two boys thrust their heads forward, started flapping their arms, and ran around in circles, cackling like birds and shouting, "WE'RE FLYING! WE'RE THE FLYING MEN!"

Soon enough, all their teammates joined in, and the next thing you knew, there were a dozen boys and girls with their arms out, flying all over the field and squawking like birds.

"Uh, I guess that's the end of the game," said the referee, a fifteen-year-old high school freshman named Edward Arthur—or was it Arthur Edwards? Whatever his exact name was, he planned on taking the twenty dollars he'd earned refereeing the game and spending it on a sausage omelet, cheese fries, and chocolate shake at the diner.

Eventually, the Anchovies players stopped flying, and families and friends of both teams congratulated all the players on a terrific game. No one seemed to care that the game had ended in a tie. The main thing was that it was now snack time.

Ben had a mouthful of cookie by the time his parents found him.

"Great game," his mom said. "You're allowed two cookies."

Ben's face fell. "Just two? I scored the tying goal!"

"You also scored two other goals," Ben's dad said.

"And one of the reasons you're scoring all these goals is because you don't eat ten cookies at halftime and another ten cookies after the game."

Ben frowned, but deep inside he was proud. Because the truth was, he always scored more goals than anyone else. And the other truth was, he was the best player on the team. By far.

"That move you put on that guy at the end," Ben's dad said, "through his legs. Have you been practicing that?"

"Not really, Dad. I just did it, I guess. Worked pretty well though, huh?"

"I'll say!"

Jay-Jay came over, with cookies in both hands. "The hero!" he crowed at Ben.

"Cut it out," Ben told his friend, but he loved it, of course.

Soon it was time to go. Lola had gotten her fair share of crumbs, but as the Cutler family walked toward their car, the never-not-hungry dog spotted one last entire, whole, glorious cookie lying on the ground in the parking lot.

So Lola did what any dog would do: she went after it.

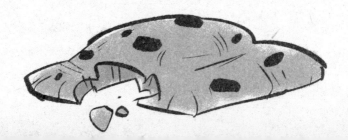

Everyone sighed with relief, and Ben's parents thanked the man over and over. The man just smiled and said, "You might want to put that dog on a leash."

"We usually do," said Ben's mom. Then she turned to her husband. "Don't we, Jim?"

Jim—Ben's dad—looked a little embarrassed because he was the one who'd forgotten to put Lola back on the leash after the game. "Absolutely," he said to his wife. Then, deciding to change the subject as quickly as possible, he turned to the man and said, "I'm not sure we've met. Do you have a kid on one of the teams?"

"I do not," the man said. "My name is James Cleary, and I coach over at the West Harbor Soccer Academy. Sometimes I come to these recreation league games to look for talent."

Ben remembered hearing somewhere that Academy soccer programs were the very highest level, but he was still a little confused. "Look for talent?" he asked. "What does that mean?"

"It means there are a lot of good players out there who can play in a more competitive environment," Mr. Cleary said. "Our program already has the best players from all over Fairville County, but I'm always looking for more talented kids to add to the team."

"So what happened today?" Ben's dad asked. "Did you find anyone?"

"I sure did."

"Oh, terrific. Who?"

Mr. Cleary smiled, then turned and looked directly at Ben.

"You."

CHAPTER THREE

LUNCHTIME DECISION

"So wait, you're like, quitting our team?"

Jay-Jay and Ben were eating lunch the next day, and Ben had just told him about meeting the Academy coach in the parking lot. Jay-Jay was eating his usual peanut butter–and–banana sandwich he'd brought from home, and Ben was eating his usual meatball hero that was the one good thing about going to school on Mondays.

"I don't know yet," Ben said. "I haven't decided. But the coach said I was good enough to play on West Harbor Academy."

"For real?"

"For real. Kinda cool, right?"

"Yeah, totally exciting," Jay-Jay answered, but Ben didn't think he sounded all that excited. In fact, Ben thought Jay-Jay sounded totally *unexcited*.

Ben tried to make his friend feel better. "I mean, I can just stay on the Anchovies though, for sure."

Jay-Jay didn't like that idea either. "No way! You're

really good at soccer, and if they want you, you gotta go play for them."

"Well, like I said, I haven't decided."

"Wait, who's on that team?" Jay-Jay asked. "Lucas McGoish plays for them, right? And Matty and Andre?"

"I think so."

Lucas McGoish was the best athlete in the grade, and Matty and Andre were his best friends. Other kids looked up to them, wanted to be them, and were annoyed by them, all at the same time.

"Just don't steal any of my goal celebrations," Jay-Jay said. "Those stay with the Anchovies."

"You got it," Ben said.

"Yo, Cutler!" said a voice behind them. "Cutler!"

Both boys turned around, and there he was: Lucas McGoish himself, heading straight toward them. Matty and Andre were a step behind. Together, the three of them looked like a rock star and his backup dancers.

"Can I get a quick bite of that?" Lucas asked, and before waiting for an answer, he chomped down half of Ben's meatball hero.

"Um . . . no?" Ben said.

Lucas narrowed his eyes. "Wait, what?"

"Just kidding."

"Oh. Ha! You're funny!"

Matty and Andre both nodded enthusiastically.

Lucas narrowed his eyes at Ben. "So, Cutler, what's this about you playing with us on West Harbor Academy?"

"You heard about that?"

Lucas snickered. "Heard about it? Dude, my dad's the assistant coach, so I know everything." He sat down, which meant that Matty and Andre did too. "Coach Cleary says you can really play. Is he right?"

"He's totally right," Jay-Jay chimed in. "Ben is an awesome player."

Lucas glanced over at Jay-Jay like he was a fly that

needed to be shooed away, then looked back at Ben. "So? You in?"

Ben took a deep breath. A voice in his head was telling him he was about to do something he would regret, but that voice was drowned out by another voice, telling him that the best athlete in his grade was asking him to join the coolest team around.

Ben nodded.

"I'm in."

CHAPTER FOUR

BEN'S NEW NICKNAME

Ben's first West Harbor Soccer Academy practice was two days later, and aside from Lucas, Matty, and Andre, he didn't recognize anyone. That wasn't surprising, though, since the team had kids from all over the county.

There weren't any girls, which was a little disappointing. Not that Ben liked girls yet or anything!! But he thought it was cool having girls on the Anchovies. They were some of the best players too.

TWEEEEEEEEETTTTTT!!! went the loudest whistle Ben had ever heard.

The man from the parking lot, Coach Cleary, was standing there with a clipboard in his hand.

"CIRCLE UP! CLEAT INSPECTION!"

Ben had no idea what that meant, until he saw all the other players turning one foot over so the coach could check the bottom of their soccer shoes.

Coach Cleary took one look at Ben's shoe and laughed. "My word, son, what is that?"

Ben was confused. "Uh, a soccer cleat?"

"Really? From what century?"

Now the rest of the team was giggling.

The coach bent down so he could talk to Ben face-to-face. "Here's the thing, lad. This is real soccer, serious soccer. In England, where I come from, we call it football, which starts with 'foot.'" He pointed with disgust at Ben's shoes. "Football is practically a religion in my country. My goal is to make it a religion here in America as well."

Ben looked down at his cleats, which suddenly looked pretty amazingly filthy.

"And so," the coach continued, "it hurts me when youngsters like yourself show up for church with equipment like that. It shows a certain lack of respect."

CLEAN CLEATS

BEN'S CLEATS

Ben hemmed and hawed. "Well, actually my parents got me these cleats just last year."

"And have you left them buried in the garden since then?"

"Uh, no?"

"And do you think it's a good reflection on your commitment to soccer to play in such dirty cleats?"

Ben could hear his new teammates start to murmur and giggle. "Probably not."

"Excellent. Then let's tidy those shoes up before next practice, fair enough?"

"Yes, sir."

"Not sir. Coach Cleary."

"Yes sir, Coach Cleary."

The coach stood back up, blew the whistle again at a deafening level, and screamed, "SHOOTING!"

Every kid except Ben knew exactly what that meant. They formed two lines, one passing line, one shooting line. Ben ran to the back of the shooting line, which moved incredibly fast. The next thing he knew, it was his turn.

"GO!" yelled the coach.

Lucas passed the ball to Ben. He took one touch, then rifled it into the upper right corner. The goalie had no chance.

"Not bad," said Lucas.

"Thanks," Ben said. Then, out of habit, he did a little

dance move on his way back into line.

Coach Cleary immediately blew his whistle. "What was that?"

"What was what?"

"Were you . . . shimmying?"

Ben shrugged. "I don't know, maybe a little."

Coach shook his head. "No no no. You're not in the Pizza League anymore, son. This is Academy soccer, the real deal. We got some of the best teams in the state in this league. Not to mention Jogo Bonito, the number one team on the entire East Coast, waiting for us in the playoffs."

"Jogo who?"

The coach scowled impatiently. "Forget about that. There's no dancing at practice. You got me, Cleatus?"

GREAT NICKNAME: "BATTLIN' BEN"

NOT SO GREAT . . . "CLEATUS"

"I got you," mumbled Ben.

Lucas guffawed. "Cleatus! He called him Cleatus!"

Everyone started laughing. "Cleatus!" they all said.

That's when Ben knew he had a new nickname, whether he liked it or not.

⚽ ⚽ ⚽

Ben cleaned his cleats the next day, but the nickname stuck. After one play at the next practice, when Ben intentionally allowed a pass to go through his legs so a teammate could get it, Coach Cleary hollered, "Well done, Cleatus, nice dummy!"

A DUMMY

Matty, who was nearby, started laughing his head off. "He just called you a dummy!"

Coach Cleary shook his head. "I did not. That play is called a dummy, and it's a brilliant strategy to fool the defender."

"Wait, for real?" Matty asked.

"For real, dummy," said Lucas.

During a break, Coach Cleary pulled Ben aside. "I like what I'm seeing. You're starting up front on Sunday."

Sunday was going to be Ben's first game with West Harbor, but the season had already started. They'd played seven games and won all seven. It was obvious to Ben that they were very, very good.

"Thank you, Coach," Ben said.

The coach nodded. "You earned it."

Lucas, who was sitting nearby taking off his shin guards, whistled and shook his head. "I'm not sure Garth is going to be too happy about that."

"Who?" asked Ben.

"Garth Wingfield. The guy whose position you're taking."

"Oh."

Lucas shrugged. "You're better than him. He'll have to deal with it."

When practice started up again, Ben found out how Garth intended to deal with it. As Ben dribbled down the

sideline during a scrimmage, Garth shoved him to the ground, hard.

"Careful there, Cleatus," grumbled Garth. "You don't want to get hurt."

Ben got to his feet and didn't say anything. He looked at Coach Cleary, waiting for him to yell at Garth. But the coach didn't even look at Garth. He just winked at Ben.

"Welcome to the Big Boy Team, son."

Ben ended up scoring three goals in the scrimmage. On the third goal, he dribbled the ball through Garth's legs before smacking it past the goalie.

"That's Mr. Cleatus to you," Ben said as he went by.

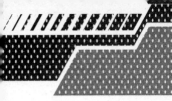

CHAPTER FIVE

THREE BIG DIFFERENCES

RED
SHIRT

BLACK
SHORTS

POLISHED
CLEATS

BLACK & RED
STRIPED
SOCKS

"Whoa," said Jay-Jay. "That's, like, the sweetest uniform I've ever seen."

"It's very nice," Ellie agreed. "I hope you shoot a lot of strikes."

Ben tried to laugh but only managed a small squeak. He was feeling a little nervous before his first Academy game, which was weird, because he had never been nervous before Pizza League games. To try to relax, he was in his room with Jay-Jay and Ellie, staring at himself in the mirror. Together, they admired the bright red shirt, the black shorts, and the black-and-red-striped high soccer socks.

Ben had to admit: he looked very, very cool.

"I'm really glad you're coming today," Ben said to Jay-Jay.

"I wouldn't miss it!" There was a slightly awkward pause, because Jay-Jay had played a Pizza League game the day before, but Ben couldn't go, because he'd had practice. It seemed like he *always* had practice.

On the way to the game, Ben's dad talked a mile a minute. "So, according to Coach Cleary, the team you're playing is really good. I guess Southgate has an all-state goalie and their striker is supposed to be very fast, so if you guys could get a good jump on them and score first it would be really important—"

"Dad?" Ellie interrupted.

"Yes, honey?"

"Can we talk about something else?"

"Anything else, actually," added Ben's mom.

Dad nodded. "Fair enough. I'm just a little excited, can you blame me? Ben's first Academy game!"

Lola, who'd had half her body out the window during most of this conversation, suddenly stuck her head back in and gave Ben's face a big slurp.

Dad let out a roar of laughter. "See? Even Lola's fired up!"

THREE IMPORTANT DIFFERENCES BETWEEN PIZZA LEAGUE GAMES AND WEST HARBOR GAMES

DIFFERENCE 1. PREGAME CHANT

ANCHOVIES CHANT:
We're the Anchovies,
   you better not bite us!
We're the Anchovies,
   you better not fight us!
We're nasty and we know
   how to win.
We're the Anchovies, so let
   the food fight begin!

WEST HARBOR CHANT:
None

After scoring his first-ever goal for West Harbor, Ben waited for his teammates to surround him, imitate him, hug him, and pound him on the back, just like all the Anchovies used to do.

And he waited some more.

And then he waited some more.

Three guys came over and gave him a quick pat on the back, and one offered a high five, but that was it. The rest of the team was already walking back into position for the kickoff.

"Get over yourself," Garth Wingfield growled in Ben's direction.

Enrico Léon was the only player who gave Ben a real smile. "Great header, Cleatus," he said.

"Thanks," Ben said. "But hold up—doesn't anyone celebrate goals around here?"

Enrico shook his head. "Coach doesn't want us to lose focus during the game. You celebrate after you win, and that's about it."

"Got it."

DIFFERENCE 2. IN-GAME CELEBRATIONS

ANCHOVIES CELEBRATIONS
- The Worm
- The Flying Man
- The Holy-Smokes-I-Can't
  Believe-I-Just-Scored
  Runaround

WEST HARBOR CELEBRATIONS
- None

With five minutes left, Ben assisted on another goal, scored by Lucas McGoish. Ben went over and offered Lucas a fist bump.

"Great shot," he said.

"Thanks," Lucas said.

"How about that pass though too, right?" Ben said. "You know, the one by me? Kind of spectacular, don't you think?"

"Huh?"

Ben grinned. "I'm just joking around."

Lucas looked at him like he had two heads.

"There's no joking around in soccer," he said.

The game ended with West Harbor winning, 3–1.

Jay-Jay came running down from the hill. "Holy moly," he said to Ben. "You can really hang with these guys!"

"I guess," Ben said, not wanting to sound too braggy.

"So how was it? Was it a blast?"

"Oh, totally. Everyone on the team is, like, so good."

Jay-Jay frowned. "Yeah, I know, but was it fun?"

Before Ben could answer, his mom arrived at the team circle with a box of blondies, Ben's absolute favorite.

"Congratulations to you all!" she said. "Since we're the new kids on the block, I thought it would be nice to bake some snacks for the boys."

But a woman swooped in and grabbed the box. "I'm sorry, but we keep the snacks healthy around here," she said. "Can't have the boys eating the wrong things with the state tournament coming up in a few weeks."

"Aha," Ben's mom said. "I see. Maybe just one each?"

"None each," said the woman.

"Mom, like, seriously?" Lucas whined. Ben couldn't help laughing a little. Of course the woman was Lucas's mom. It made total sense.

Someone's dad took out a tin of banana slices, which were handed out to all.

Ellie scrunched up her nose. "Ew."

"Yikes, this is no joke," said Ben's dad.

Even Lola looked crushed.

Ben ruffled her fur. "I know," Ben moaned. "I can't believe it either."

DIFFERENCE 3. POSTGAME SNACK

ANCHOVIES SNACKS:
- Cupcakes
- Cookies
- Cake
- Those cheesy swirly thingies

WEST HARBOR SNACKS:
- Fruit
- Carrot sticks
- More fruit
- More carrot sticks

CHAPTER SIX

SOLARMAN IS GONNA HAVE TO WAIT

In the next four weeks, Ben had nine practices, six games, twelve orange slices, nine sticks of celery, seven mistakes that made the coach yell at him, four goals, and zero goal celebrations.

West Harbor won every game, bringing their final regular-season record to thirteen wins and no losses. The team was among the favorites to win the state tournament, which was coming up. But Coach Cleary wanted to make sure his team didn't get overconfident.

"You guys are good, but you're not *that* good!" the coach yelled one day, as the team ran laps around the field during practice. "You're no Jogo Bonito!"

Ben rolled his eyes at the mention of Jogo Bonito. Coach Cleary talked about them all the time, and West Harbor hadn't even played them yet.

"That team from upstate, Jogo Bonito, is pretty near unbeatable," he'd say.

Or, "They've been practicing six days a week since they were five years old. "These guys are for real."

Or, "The Jogo Bonito guys are massive. They never lose. They don't mess around."

Or, "Jogo Bonito means 'the beautiful game' in Portuguese, the language they speak in Brazil. Pelé was from Brazil. He called soccer the beautiful game. That's all you need to know."

Ben thought the coach was kind of obsessed with Jogo Bonito, to be honest.

PELÉ: THE GREATEST SOCCER PLAYER EVER

The night before the first game of the tournament, Ben and his family went to their favorite pizza-and-salad restaurant, Slice and Dice. They used to go there after every Pizza League game, but it had been a while.

"I'd like to propose a toast," said Ben's dad. "To Ben,

who has quickly become one of the best players on the best soccer team in the whole state."

"Dad!" protested Ben. "You're embarrassing me."

"Why? I'm just saying what's true. You're a great soccer player."

Ben shook his head. "It's not that. It's that you're toasting with *water*. Everyone knows that the only drink that goes with pizza is root beer."

"I agree!" pronounced Ellie.

Ben's dad smacked his forehead in pretend horror. "Oh my gosh!" he cried out. "You're absolutely right! Waiter, get me some root beer, STAT!"

"*Stat?*" asked Ben.

"That's medical talk for immediately," Ben's mom explained.

Once order had been restored, Ben's dad tried again. "Where was I before I was so rudely interrupted? Oh, right—Ben's a great soccer player, blah blah blah, yadda yadda, cheers."

"Perfect!" squealed Ellie.

"Thanks, Dad," Ben said.

The family started dividing up the meatball-and-artichoke pizza. "Seriously kid, we're so proud of you," Dad said. "The coach has been really impressed—in fact, he asked me the other day if you want to go to his summer camp this year. He said it's highly selective. Kids come from all over the tristate area—it's a big deal."

Ellie plucked the artichokes off her slice and put them on her mom's plate, the way she always did. "Can I go to sleepaway camp?" she asked. "Jenny's older sister went, and she said she kissed a boy there."

"Well, in that case, you can absolutely go," said Ben's mom. "As soon as you turn eighteen."

"Ha-ha," Ellie said, her mouth full of meatballs.

"So whaddya say?" Ben's dad asked Ben. "How lucky are you, right?"

Ben nodded. "I'm so lucky."

Ben knew it was a great opportunity—a lot of kids would love to go to a camp like that—but for some reason he wasn't all that excited about it. Maybe it was because he knew that every day at soccer camp meant one less day hanging out at the beach eating ice-cream sandwiches.

"Cool," said Ben's dad. "I'll let the coach know."

Ben was diving into his second slice when he heard a voice behind him.

"Cutler! Yo, Cutler!"

Ben turned around to see Lucas McGoish heading his way, with his dad right next to him.

Ben's dad got up to greet them, so Ben did the same.

"Funny meeting you guys here," Coach McGoish said in a booming voice. "I guess this is where all the soccer studs have their pregame meals, huh?"

Lucas smacked Ben on the back. "Yo, Matty and Andre are coming over tomorrow night for a sleepover after the game. Hopefully a few of the other guys too. You in?"

Ben thought for a second. "Tomorrow night?" There was something in the back of his mind that he was trying to remember, something else he was supposed to do the next night, but he couldn't think of what it was. "Uh, sure, Lucas, sounds great, thanks."

Lucas winked. "Of course, if we lose, the whole thing's off, but we're not going to lose, no way, no how. Not with you and me dominating up front, am I right?"

Uh-oh . . .

"You're totally right," Ben said.

They slapped hands, which Ben thought kind of hurt.

"Cool, Cleatus. Anyway, I gotta go chomp my pie."

As they watched Lucas and his father go back to their table, Ben's mom said, "Cleatus?"

"Long story," mumbled Ben.

Ellie asked, "Who was that guy?"

"That was Lucas," Ben answered. "Lucas McGoish."

"Is he your friend?"

"I guess so. He's on the soccer team."

"Oh."

"Why do you ask?"

Ellie shrugged. "Because he seems kind of obnoxious."

"Also," said Ben's mom, "aren't you supposed to go to the new SolarMan movie with Jay-Jay tomorrow night?"

Ben slapped his forehead. "Dang it! I knew I forgot something!"

"Well, you can tell Lucas you forgot that you already had plans," Ben's mom said.

Ben knew it wasn't going to be that simple. Lucas wasn't exactly the type of guy you said no to. Especially if you said yes first.

"Do you want another slice, Ben?" asked his dad.

But suddenly Ben wasn't very hungry anymore.

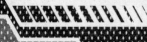

CHAPTER SEVEN

THE PHONE CALL

Hey, everyone, Freddy here . . . We've got a real tense one on our hands, with Ben trying to get himself out of a sticky situation . . .

Whoa, looks like he's gonna go old-school on us and make an actual phone call!

Let's see how this plays out . . .

"Hi, Ms. Wright, is Jay-Jay there?"
"Oh, hi, Ben! Yep sure, hold on just a sec."
"Hello?"
"Hey, Jay-Jay, it's me."

"Hey."

"What's up?"

"So, uh, not much . . . uh, are you coming to the game today?"

"Your playoff game?"

"Yeah."

"Oh, uh, I don't think so. It's kind of far away—like, I'm not sure my parents can drive me."

"Oh, well, uh, you can come with us if you want."

"That would be cool, but I think I have to go visit my aunt anyway."

"Oh, got it, cool, okay."

"But I'll see you later though, right? The movie is at seven thirty. Maybe you can come over for dinner first?"

"Oh, yeah, I mean, uh, I guess the thing is, I forgot I have this other thing."

"You have another thing?"

"Yeah, uh, a soccer thing. There's a sleepover at Lucas's house with some kids from the team."

"Oh. Which kids?"

"Uh, Matty and Andre and some other kids."

"Matty and Andre?"

"Yeah."

"I thought, like, you didn't really like those guys."

"They're okay, I guess. And, you know, they're on the team and stuff."

"Oh, yeah, right. Okay. So, um, then, I guess we can go to the movie another time."

"Yeah, absolutely."

"Maybe next weekend."

"Definitely."

"Okay."

"Oh wait, Jay-Jay . . . do you have a game this weekend?"

"Yeah, our last game."

"Oh, cool. Maybe I can come."

"Oh sweet, yeah, that'd be cool."

"Okay."

"Great."

"Uh, okay, bye."

"Bye."

Well, there you have it! A fine gestu[r] by Jay-Jay offering to reschedule th[e] movie, and an excellent save by Ber[t] offering to go to Jay-Jay's game. Those are the kinds of in-game decisions that are so important to becoming successful human being[s] Well played, fellas!

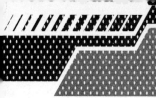

CHAPTER EIGHT
THE TWO MINUTES THAT CHANGED EVERYTHING

The first tournament game was against Medford Heights, a town Ben had never heard of. It was way upstate, and during the car ride there, Ben's father listened to a podcast about soccer in England.

Ben's mom, however, did not care about soccer in England. "Jim, do we really have to listen to this?"

Dad laughed. "Sorry, hon. Just for a few more minutes. It's really fascinating how soccer is like a religion over there."

"My coach said that once," said Ben.

Ben's dad turned onto the highway. "And you know they call it football, right?"

"Well aware," said Mom. Then she added, "Remember back when you weren't a huge soccer nut, hon? I mean, football?"

"I have no idea what you're talking about," Dad said, chuckling.

"It was a month ago!"

"Well, people change, hon."

"They sure do," Ben's mom said, and that was the last thing Ben heard before he fell asleep.

⚽ ⚽ ⚽

WEST HARBOR VS. MEDFORD HEIGHTS

Fifteen minutes into the game, Medford Heights scored the only goal of the first half, when one of their strikers fired a low shot from just outside the penalty area, and goalkeeper Billy Clay couldn't quite reach it. At halftime, West Harbor was behind for the first time since Ben had joined the team. And Coach Cleary was not happy.

"BOYS!" he hollered. "What's going on out there? Did everyone sleep on the car ride up here?"

I did, thought Ben.

"Well if you did, it looks like you FORGOT TO WAKE UP!" the coach ranted. "These guys aren't half as good as Jogo Bonito, and you're making them look like the French national team!"

Ben was only half listening. The other part of his brain was thinking about how fun halftime used to be at the Anchovies games, when the kids would be goofing around, and one of the parents would bring over juice boxes. Boy, those were delicious.

The coach was just getting warmed up. "I need you boys to get it together, fast! We need to lock down their strikers, distribute from midfield, and attack relentlessly. Can you boys do that? Because if you can't, there are a lot of other kids out there who would be happy to work hard for me! SO SHOW ME YOU WANT IT!"

"Let's get after it!" yelled Lucas's dad, who was the assistant coach, even though Coach Cleary didn't really let him do anything. "Show us what you're made of! You got this!"

Ben and his teammates kept their heads down while listening to their coaches. Ben suddenly felt so anxious he wasn't even sure his legs were going to work. But he would find out soon enough, because the second half was about to begin.

DOINK! And it hits the crossbar! No goal! West Harbor just barely escapes! They could easily be down two goals right now . . .

There's Ben Cutler, one of West Harbor's strikers, giving Billy Clay a pat on the back.

Great save!

Hah, that's a good one! Billy obviously didn't make the save, his crossbar did! Ben seems to be trying to loosen things up, help the team relax into the game . . . let's see if it works . . .

Yes! It seems like that lucky break and Ben Cutler's joke were enough to settle the whole team down . . . they've been playing much better in the last few minutes . . .

When Lucas scored the tying goal, the crowd on the West Harbor side went nuts, and all the players actually celebrated—a little. They met in front of the goal in a group hug, and screamed "YEAH!" at one another, for about five seconds.

The team had turned a corner. West Harbor started to dominate, and Medford Heights was back on their heels, but neither team could score. The clock wound down: fifteen minutes left . . . ten minutes left . . . five minutes left . . .

"IF THERE'S ONE THING I HATE, IT'S A TIE!" screamed Lucas. "NO TIES! LET'S WIN THIS THING!!"

fires it upfield to Lucas McGoish . . . Lucas spots Ben Cutler streaking down the middle of the field . . .

There was an explosion of noise from the crowd. The whole team mobbed Ben, and everyone was screaming at the top of their lungs.

"WE DID IT!" screamed Andre.

"I CAN'T BELIEVE IT!" screamed Matty.

Even Garth Wingfield, who usually made it a point to be mean to Ben, screamed, "THIS IS AWESOME!"

The crowd noise, the team noise, the fact that the game was basically over—all of it got Ben so excited that before he knew it, he did the one thing he was told never, ever, *ever* to do.

He danced.

Not only did he dance—he broke out the majordomo, the big kahuna, the special-occasion-numero-uno dance— The Flying Man. Up went the arms, waving wildly, as Ben hopped around, yapping and flapping, living in the moment, finally enjoying himself and feeling like he belonged.

It felt amazing!

Until it didn't.

That was some goal! Ben Cutler has run over to his team's sideline and is dancing up a storm out there . . .

Ben saw the play happen as if it were in slow motion, as he desperately ran down the field. The Medford Heights player shooting . . . Billy Clay diving for the ball and missing . . . And Lucas McGoish making a game-saving play, then smacking into the goalpost.

And the whole time, Ben was thinking one thing.

I messed up.

The team surrounded Lucas, congratulating him and making sure he was okay. Lucas got up slowly, holding his nose and screaming, "OOOWWWWW!"

Then the blood started coming, and Lucas started crying. "THIS IS ALL CLEATUS'S FAULT!" he wailed. "HE WAS TOO BUSY DANCING TO HELP OUT ON DEFENSE AND THEY ALMOST SCORED AND I BROKE MY FACE!"

Everyone stared at Ben as he sat down on the bench, stunned. Two minutes earlier, he'd been the hero—and now, his teammates were looking at him like he'd just kicked a puppy.

Ben's family came over to see him on the bench, but he waved them away, wanting to be alone. But he wasn't alone for long.

Coach Cleary came over and sat down right next to him. The coach didn't say anything for a few seconds, and Ben thought maybe he was trying to come up with just the right words to make him feel better. But when the coach finally spoke, his words did NOT make Ben feel better. At all.

"I talked to you about this," Coach Cleary said, in a scary whisper. "We have a rule against excessive celebration of goals. And you broke that rule. As a result, you almost cost us the game and got one of our best players injured. Maybe now you will realize that actions have consequences. And irresponsible actions have bad consequences."

Ben could feel his whole body getting hot, and a tear started to form at the edge of his right eye.

"Don't be late for practice on Tuesday," Coach Cleary said. Then he got up and left without another word.

When Ben's parents came over to see if he was ready to leave, he refused to look at them.

He did look at Lola, however. She jumped up and put her giant paws on Ben's lap. He hugged her and actually smiled for a second.

Dogs are like that.

CHAPTER NINE
HALFTIME VISITOR

Needless to say, the sleepover at Lucas's house was canceled. And the next day, Ben didn't feel like doing much of anything.

"No thanks," he said, when his dad asked him if he wanted breakfast.

"Not right now," he said, when his mom asked him if he wanted to throw the Frisbee around.

"Maybe later," he said, when his sister asked him if he wanted to watch a hilarious YouTube video of a surfing goat.

Then Jay-Jay called.

"You're still coming today, right?"

Ben had totally forgotten about Jay-Jay's game. It was the Anchovies against the Green Peppers, and it was the last game of the Pizza League season.

Ben's first instinct was to say no. He was definitely not in the mood to go anywhere near a soccer field if he didn't have to, and had been planning on spending the day feeling sorry for himself.

But he wasn't about to let his best friend down either. Not again.

"Sure thing," Ben said. "I'll meet you there."

The game was at eleven, and by the time Ben's mom dropped him at the field, his mood had improved slightly, thanks to the chocolate chip pancakes his dad had made, even though Ben said he didn't want them.

Jay-Jay—who was in the middle of a contest with his teammates to see who could balance a ball on their noses the longest—ran over to say hi.

"Hey guess what," Jay-Jay said. "As soon as I score, I'm breaking out a new move. I'm calling it the Moondance."

"Whoa," said Ben. "What is it?"

"You'll see."

Ben waved to his former teammates on the Anchovies. Then he looked across the field to see if he knew any kids on the Green Peppers. He saw Elgin, his seatmate in the clarinet section of the band, and Gerald, the kid who always ate an egg sandwich on the way to school, making the whole bus smell kind of gross.

Then Ben noticed Annabella Donatello. Annabella was a really nice girl who lived on Ben's street, and they were friendly with each other, but not quite friends. In fact, Ben had no idea Annabella played soccer. But here she was, in her bright green uniform, her long black hair tied back in a ponytail, doing a passing drill with the rest of the Peppers.

Ben heard the Anchovies coach, Mr. Song, say what he always said before games: "Go have fun out there!"

TWO MORE IMPORTANT DIFFERENCES BETWEEN PIZZA LEAGUE GAMES AND WEST HARBOR GAMES

WEST HARBOR SKILL LEVEL	PIZZA LEAGUE SKILL LEVEL
• High	• Not so high

WEST HARBOR	PIZZA LEAGUE
STRESS LEVEL	STRESS LEVEL
• High	• Not so high

It turned out the Pizza League was full of kids who didn't really know how to play soccer. The passing was sloppy, there wasn't a lot of communication on the field, and the ball was constantly going out-of-bounds, because no one knew how to kick it with any accuracy.

But guess what? It didn't matter. Someone would make a bad pass, and no one would get mad. Someone would kick the ball out-of-bounds, and no one would scream. The coaches encouraged the players, sure, but they didn't yell at them. Everyone wanted to score, and win, but it didn't feel like a matter of life and death.

Even the parents on the sidelines didn't seem nervous about the game. And parents were *always* nervous whenever their kids did *anything*.

Ben cheered for Jay-Jay, but the truth was, without Ben out there to help him, Jay-Jay wasn't much better than anyone else. As Ben watched his friend run around— smiling, laughing, and trying his hardest—Ben realized that Jay-Jay was doing something that Ben had forgotten was even possible on a soccer field.

He was playing soccer . . . with the emphasis on *PLAY*.

Meanwhile, Ben was also keeping a close eye on Annabella. It turned out that she was one of the best players out there. Annabella played defense and had a big booming kick that sent the ball all the way down the field. And whenever the Anchovies had the ball near the Green Peppers goal, Annabella was right there to clear it out of danger.

At halftime, the score was tied, 0–0. Ben went down to see Jay-Jay and the rest of his old teammates, and immediately noticed a bag of juice boxes sitting on the grass. It looked like there were two or three left over.

DRINK ME!

"Hey, is it okay if I grab one of these?" Ben asked, to no one in particular. A few kids shrugged, which Ben took as a yes, so he sat down on the bench and helped himself. It tasted absolutely delicious.

A boy named Charlie, who wore athletic glasses that looked like goggles, plopped down next to Ben. "Hey, Ben, how's West Harbor Academy going? Is it, like, so sick?"

"Oh yeah, totally sick," Ben said. "We're undefeated. It's awesome."

"That's so cool," said Charlie. "I always knew you were like, too good for us."

Ben shook his head. "I'm not too good for you guys. The Anchovies are the best. I miss being on the team."

"Yeah, sure," Charlie said, not believing Ben for a second.

Jay-Jay joined them on the bench. "Dang, Ben, I can't get past that girl Annabella," he whined. "She's tough back there."

"She is," Ben agreed. "You have to stay away from her. Instead of going down the middle every time, go left. The kid that plays over there can be beaten. Then if you cut in, you should be able to get right to the goal."

Jay-Jay nodded in appreciation. "Wow. You're, like, a soccer genius."

Before Ben could respond, he heard a girl's voice behind him.

"Are you guys talking about me?"

And there she was. Annabella Donatello, standing there with her hands on her hips.

"Uh . . ." Jay-Jay said. "What . . ."

Annabella scrunched up her eyes a little bit. "Hey, Ben, hey, Jay-Jay. My coach asked me to see if you had an extra ice pack. Someone on our team has a sore foot and ours are starting to melt."

Every Anchovies player immediately scattered to find ice, which left Ben sitting there, alone. Annabella peered down at him. "But then I heard my name mentioned, so I was like, are they talking about me?"

Ben smiled and shrugged. "We were just saying what a good soccer player you were."

Annabella grinned. "Oh, cool! Thanks!"

Charlie and Jay-Jay came back with an ice pack, which Annabella took with a friendly smile. "See you guys out there!" she said. Before she ran back to her team's bench, she paused to boot one of the Anchovies' practice balls practically to the moon.

"Sheesh," Jay-Jay said.

"Remember to go left," Ben said.

CHAPTER TEN

WHAT'S A TACKLE?

The defensive battle continued into the second half, and the score was still 0–0 as the clock ticked away toward the final whistle.

Jay-Jay had totally forgotten about Ben's advice. He kept trying to dribble down the middle of the field, and every time, Annabella was there to distract, disrupt, or dislodge the ball from Jay-Jay's feet.

"GO LEFT!" Ben screamed over and over again. But Jay-Jay was in a world of his own, and Ben finally gave up.

Then, with about six minutes left, Mr. Song's daughter, a midfielder named Erica, sent the ball down the field. A Green Peppers player wound up and took a mighty swing, but only managed to connect with one small corner of the ball, sending it sideways, directly to Jay-Jay's feet. He looked up and saw open field in front of him.

"GO!" yelled all his teammates.

So he went.

Jay-Jay Wright charging down the middle of the field with the ball . . .

here comes Annabella Donatello out to challenge . . .

Ernie, who'd spent most of the game thinking about the episode of the *LightningStriker* TV show he'd watched that morning, suddenly realized that Jay-Jay was heading right toward him.

"Tackle him, Ernie!" urged Annabella. "You got this! Tackle the ball away from him!"

The problem was, Ernie didn't realize that in soccer, "tackle" means to kick the ball away from an opponent. Ernie was only familiar with the American football definition of "tackle." So Ernie wrapped his arms around Jay-Jay and bear-hugged him until they both tumbled to the ground.

FOOTBALL TACKLE

SOCCER TACKLE

Uh-oh! That's got to be a penalty kick!

Yup, the referee has blown her whistle. Penalty kick it is!

The Anchovies players jumped up and down with excitement. Ernie, who was both confused and disappointed, was quickly consoled by his fellow Green Peppers, including Annabella, who slapped Ernie's shoulder and said, "My bad, buddy! I shouldn't have said 'tackle.' Not your fault!"

Mr. Song pointed at Jay-Jay. "You earned the penalty," he announced. "You take the kick."

"Me?" Jay-Jay suddenly felt a jolt of excitement shoot through his body. "Wait, for real?"

"For real," said Mr. Song, who knew only slightly more about soccer than Ernie Clompston did. "Just stay calm, and remember, it's no big deal—whatever happens, happens. Although what I would very much like to happen is you putting the ball in the goal, so our team can be victorious, and I can win a bet with my wife that the Anchovies will win more than three games this season." Then he winked and added, "No pressure."

The referee handed the ball to Jay-Jay, who placed it on the penalty spot. From where he was watching, Ben assumed Jay-Jay was freaking out a little bit. *Stay calm,* Ben thought. *You got this.*

But then Jay-Jay turned, looked up at Ben, and shouted, "DUDE! REMEMBER WHAT I SAID!" It took Ben a few seconds to remember that Jay-Jay had told him he was going to show off a new dance if he scored. At first Ben was amazed that Jay-Jay was relaxed enough to think about that, but then he remembered this was a Pizza League game. You didn't have to feel nervous in a Pizza League game.

Jay-Jay stared down at the ball, then ran up and kicked it right into the corner of the goal.

It's in the net! Jay-Jay Wright just hit a perfect penalty kick!

The crowd is going wild as Jay-Jay launches into a celebration dance that

The crowd went wild as all the Anchovies mobbed Jay-Jay. Meanwhile, Jay-Jay was still jumping around the field in giant steps. It was the Moondance! Ben had to admit, Jay-Jay looked just like one of those astronauts taking big, gravity-defying leaps on the surface of the moon.

The next thing you knew, Jay-Jay's Anchovies teammates started doing the Moon dance too, and all of a sudden there were a bunch of kids jumping around the field. Then the Green Peppers kids started doing it too! Soon it became a contest to see who could jump the farthest. Annabella Donatello won by a mile.

THE MOONDANCE

The game ended 1–0, and after the final whistle, Ben ran down to celebrate with his old teammates on the sideline.

"What a great penalty kick!" Ben told Jay-Jay.

But Jay-Jay was more interested in talking about his dance. "What did you think of my spaceman moves? Pretty cool, right?"

"Very cool," Ben said.

"You can steal it if you want."

"Ha. I'd probably be kicked off West Harbor Academy if I did."

Jay-Jay shook his head. "Ah, boo them."

Ben had to admit, his friend had a point.

The cupcakes came out two minutes later, right on schedule. Today, they were chocolate with butterscotch frosting. Ben was hoping there might be a few extra. There were, and Mr. Song offered one to Ben.

It tasted a lot better than banana slices.

CHAPTER ELEVEN
A WEEK AT SCHOOL

The next week in school was not much fun for Ben. Lucas McGoish made sure of that.

On Monday at lunch, Lucas went around the cafeteria announcing to everyone who would listen that the reason he had a swollen nose and two black eyes was because Ben Cutler was more interested in dancing than playing soccer.

On Tuesday in gym class, Lucas showed everyone the Flying Man dance, but he did it in a way that made the dance look like the most ridiculous thing in the world.

On Wednesday at recess, Lucas, Matty, and Andre put on giant hockey masks when they were picked to be on the same basketball team as Ben.

Nothing embarrassing happened on Thursday.

On Friday after school, Lucas invented a song that went, *Ben Cutler doesn't care if you win or lose, he just wants to wear his dancing shoes. Ben Cutler doesn't care if you break your nose, as long as he can dance on his tippy toes!*

Ben had to admit, the song was pretty clever. But that didn't make it any more enjoyable when the entire school bus started singing it.

79

CHAPTER TWELVE
A MISSION, AND A DECISION

Hey everyone, I've got some shocking news! It's the semifinals of the state tournament, a must win for West Harbor Academy, and their newest superstar, striker Ben Cutler, isn't in the starting lineup!

I wonder what's going on . . .

During pregame warm-ups, Coach Cleary called Ben over to talk. "So listen, we're going to go with Lucas, Enrico, and Garth up top. Just changing things up. But be ready, I'll need you to be a real spark plug when you go in."

Ben knew exactly why he wasn't starting: Coach Cleary was punishing him for the goal celebration and making an example out of him. Ben decided that when his time came, he would show everyone how well he'd learned his lesson.

"Okay, Coach," Ben said. "Sure thing."

As the game started, Lucas, who had a protective mask on his face, played well, but Garth was struggling. He missed a couple of clear goal-scoring opportunities, and after a third shot clonked off his shin, the coach motioned to Ben. "Go in for Garth."

Garth had already lost his starting position to Ben when Ben first joined the team, and he sure wasn't happy to be coming out of the game now. "Don't hurt anybody, Dancing Cleatus," he growled. But Ben didn't let it bother him. He wasn't going to let anything distract him from his mission: to play well and to mind his own business.

dribbles past one defender,

sweeps out wide and sends a long, perfect ball into the box . . . and Lucas McGoish slots it home! 1–0, West Harbor!

As soon as the ball went in the net, Ben ran back to his position, waiting for kickoff. Lucas, who was accepting congratulations from his teammates, finally noticed him standing there. "Nice cross, Cleatus."

Ben nodded.

Lucas frowned. "What, so now you're all, like, a robot or something?"

Ben said nothing.

"Whatever," said Lucas.

Ben scored another goal in the second half, and assisted on one more, before coming out of the game with ten minutes to go. After the game, which West Harbor won 5–1, Coach Cleary gathered the team in a circle for the postgame talk. The first thing he did was look straight at Ben.

"Well, Cleatus, you were nasty out there today," said Coach Cleary. "Great game. We got Jogo Bonito in the finals. I don't need to tell you how tough a game that will be. I need you focused, just like today."

"Got it," said Ben.

The coach smiled, satisfied that he had finally gotten through to his new star player, and that everything was going to be smooth sailing from now on.

When Ben's parents congratulated him after the game, he barely looked at them. Then he said one sentence.

"I want to quit soccer."

CHAPTER THIRTEEN

HOW MUCH POWER DOES ICE CREAM REALLY HAVE?

The hot fudge sundae was making Ben feel better, but only a little.

He was sitting with his parents, his sister, and his very hungry dog, Lola, on a bench outside the Scooper Dooper Ice Cream Shoppe, trying to explain why he didn't want to play for West Harbor Soccer Academy anymore.

"I don't know, I guess it's just not for me," he said between bites. "I should feel excited and everything to be on this team, I know it's an honor and stuff, but like, I just miss being on the Anchovies."

"Because . . . ?" asked his mom.

"I don't know, I just liked it better."

"Is it the coach?" asked his dad. "He does seem pretty intense."

"It's everything. Yeah, the coach is totally serious all the time, but it's, like, even the other kids act like they're in the pros. And the parents are so nervous and uptight on the sideline, we can feel it on the field. It just makes everything way more stressful."

"It's a dumb soccer game!" said Ellie. "Who cares?"

Ben shrugged. "A lot of people, as it turns out." He finished off his sundae, then let Lola take a few licks of the bowl. "I know I messed up last game, when I thought the game was over and I was celebrating. But in the Pizza League, people don't make you feel like a loser if you lose, or like you're the worst person in the world if you make one mistake."

Ben's parents looked at each other.

"Tough to argue with that," his dad said. "But there's only one game left. How about playing in that game, and we'll go from there. Does that seem fair?"

Ben thought about it for a few seconds, then realized that quitting right before the championship game would really let his teammates down.

"Yeah, I guess," he said.

"You're so talented at soccer," said Ben's mom. "It would be a shame for you to quit. You go play your heart out, show them how good you are, and then we'll figure it out, I promise."

"Okay, Mom." Ben felt a little better, having talked about it, but he wasn't sure his parents were taking him that seriously. If he wasn't having fun playing soccer, he didn't want to play.

It was as simple as that.

CHAPTER FOURTEEN

A DEAL AT LUNCH

The next day at lunch, Annabella Donatello walked up to Ben and Jay-Jay's table for the first time ever.

"Can I sit here?" she said, right after she sat down.

Ben and Jay-Jay looked at each other. "Sure," they said at the same exact time.

"Cool, thanks," Annabella said. She took a big bite of her chicken salad sandwich. "So, what are you guys up to?"

Ben was busy chewing, so Jay-Jay said, "Actually, Annabella, Ben was just telling me he doesn't want to play for West Harbor Academy anymore."

"For real?" asked Annabella. "That's bonkers!"

"I don't know," Ben said. "I'm thinking about it."

Annabella helped herself to one of Jay-Jay's french fries. "What's the problem? I mean, isn't that, like, where all the best kids play? I was actually thinking about trying out for the West Harbor girls' team."

"You totally should," Jay-Jay said. "You're really good."

"Yeah, you're really, really good," Ben agreed.

Annabella smiled. "Thanks, you guys. I just started playing soccer last year, but already it's my favorite sport, besides softball."

"That's awesome," Jay-Jay said.

"Yeah, that's super awesome," Ben said. He was fully aware that he was just repeating everything Jay-Jay said.

"So why would you want to quit?" Annabella asked Ben. "Don't you love soccer?"

"I think I love soccer, yeah. I just don't love being on this team," Ben said. "I don't know. I guess it's hard to explain."

Jay-Jay stepped in. "He thinks it's too intense."

"Ha!" Annabella said, snorting out a laugh, but then she realized Jay-Jay was serious. "Wait, for real? Soccer *is* intense! That's what's great about it! You go out there, and you want to win, and you play super hard, and you're mad if you do bad and happy if you do well, and it's awesome, right?"

Annabella was making a lot of sense, which made Ben more confused than ever. "But . . . I just liked being on the Anchovies more."

She laughed again. "Ben, the Pizza League is for people who want to run around and goof off and don't really care. If you're playing Academy soccer, that's, like, a big deal, so of course it's more serious."

"Jeez Louise," Ben said, because he had no idea what else to say.

Annabella finished off her sandwich, took a long swig of chocolate milk, and then announced, "Hey, I know!" She smacked her hand down on the table, rattling everyone's trays. "Instead of moaning and groaning about how you don't want to play on the Academy team anymore because they're so mean and serious, how about doing something about it?"

"I never said they were mean," Ben mumbled.

"Great idea, Annabella!" Jay-Jay said. "We could figure out a way to make them less annoying!"

"I never said they were annoying," Ben mumbled.

Annabella looked confused. "So what's the problem, then?"

"I just want it to be more fun, that's all. It's not a big deal. The championship game is this weekend, and then the season's over and I'll figure it out."

Annabella's eyes went wide. "You guys are in the *championship* game?? Oh, boo hoo!!"

Ben sighed. He was tired of talking about it. It all seemed so simple, but so complicated at the same time.

The bell rang, signaling the end of lunch.

"Okay, so here's what we're going to do," Annabella announced. "Jay-Jay and I are gonna come to the game and watch you suffer through being on the best soccer team in the whole state. If you win we'll go out for ice cream, and if you lose we'll never talk to you again. Deal?"

Ben looked at Annabella, trying to figure out if she was kidding or serious. He ended up deciding she was being a little of both.

"Deal," he said.

CHAPTER FIFTEEN

A ROUGH START

It's championship Sunday, people . . . the day we've all been waiting for!

Drumroll

"Cleatus, you're back in the starting lineup," Coach Cleary said during warm-ups. "You played extremely well in the last game, keep it up."

"Yes, Coach." Ben was happy to be starting, but he was also distracted, because he was staring across the field. There they were: the opponents. The bad guys. The dangerous, six-practices-a-week, legendary Jogo Bonito Academy.

The two scariest words in the English language: Jogo Bonito! (Actually, it's not the English language. It's Portuguese.)

Ben watched the Jogo Bonito players go through their drills, and he noticed one surprising thing right away: they were smiling. In fact, they were laughing and joking around as they raced around the field, dribbling and passing and shooting with perfect precision.

The two happiest words in the English language: Jogo Bonito!

Then the game began, and Jogo Bonito was on fire. West Harbor Academy, on the other hand, was not.

What's going on out there, folks? The West Harbor players look like they're stuck in mud. Are they nervous? Tired? Whatever it is, they need to turn things around, and fast . . .

Ben couldn't believe it. No one could believe it. They were sloppy, they were making mistakes, and worst of all, they were snapping at each other for making those mistakes. Meanwhile, Jogo Bonito kept whipping the ball around, finding the open man, encouraging each other, and looking calm and confident.

During one pause in the action, Coach Cleary called his players over to the sideline. "What's going on out there?" he demanded. "You guys are playing like you think you don't deserve to be here!"

"BILLY!" screamed Lucas. "WHAT WAS THAT? ARE YOU KIDDING ME?"

"DO YOU WANT TO PLAY GOALIE?" Billy screamed back. "BE MY GUEST!"

"MAYBE I SHOULD!" hollered Lucas.

Billy Clay started to cry, but he stopped quickly, when the Jogo Bonito player who scored came over and patted him on the shoulder.

"COME ON, GUYS, GET YOUR HEADS OUT OF YOUR—" shouted Coach Cleary, before remembering that he was coaching children.

But nothing was working. The team was totally over-matched, and Jogo Bonito scored another goal just before halftime. This one was nobody's fault. It was just an amazing shot by a Jogo Bonito player, who celebrated with a dance that involved a shoulder shimmy, a hip shake, and two backflips.

Ben was impressed with both the goal and the celebration. At the center line, he asked the goal scorer, "Do you have a name for that dance?"

"Nah," the boy said. "I just make it up as I go along."

"It was sweet."

"Thanks." The Jogo Bonito guy gave Ben a friendly smile. "You're a really good player, by the way."

"Thanks a lot," Ben said, but before he could say anything else, the referee blew his whistle.

"HALFTIME!"

The boy ran by Ben on his way to his bench. He tapped Ben on the shoulder. "My name's Diego. What's yours?"

"Ben," Ben said.

Diego grinned again. "Good luck in the second half!"

Ben nodded. "Same!"

On his way over to the bench, he realized something. Coach was right about how good the Jogo Bonito players were.

But he was wrong about the scary part.

CHAPTER SIXTEEN
A HALFTIME TO REMEMBER

The team gathered in a circle at halftime, listening to Coach Cleary as he tried not to lose his temper.

"Well," he said. "That was . . . uh, I don't even really know how to describe what that was. It was terrible. It was HORRIBLE. IT WAS AWFUL!" Then he managed to calm himself down, slightly. "But it's over. It's behind us. We're down two, but we have a whole half left. Let's put that out of our minds, and go out there, and play the kind of soccer we know we're capable of playing. Whaddya say, boys?"

The boys said, well, nothing. They just sat on the grass, sipping their waters and fancy sports drinks, still trying to understand what had gone wrong.

Ben, meanwhile, sat on the outer ring of the circle the way he always did, so he could be farther away from the coach's tantrums. Looking up at the crowd, he saw Jay-Jay and Annabella and shrugged as if to say, *Whaddya gonna do?*

"Remember!" Annabella yelled. "If you lose, I'm never speaking to you again!" But she was laughing while she said it.

Ben nodded at his parents, who looked pretty stressed-out. But Ellie, who was holding Lola on a leash, looked like she didn't have a care in the world.

"Hi, Ben!" she yelled, grinning and waving. "Score a basket!"

Coach Cleary wound up his halftime talk with a big finish. "As the great FDR once said, 'The only thing we have to fear is fear itself.' So let's go out there and stop playing like scared little boys!!"

Ben's teammates tried to look as excited as possible. But Ben wasn't excited. He was too busy thinking about how the Jogo Bonito guys actually seemed pretty nice, and about Annabella's joke, and about his anxious parents, and his nervous teammates, and about how fun halftime was at the Anchovies games, with juice boxes and cupcakes.

And then Ben thought about Ellie smiling and saying he should score a basket, and he had two reactions.

First, he laughed.

And then, he decided he had something to say.

Ben raised his hand. "Excuse me, Coach Cleary?" he said. "I think I know why we've been playing like scared little boys."

The coach narrowed his eyes at Ben. "And why's that?"

"Because you told us to."

Ben's teammates slowly turned their heads toward him, as if he were an alien.

"You've been telling us all season how terrifying Jogo Bonito are, which is probably why we came out here terrified," Ben explained. "And yeah, they're a great team, but it turns out they're not that terrifying. They actually seem like really nice kids who just love to play soccer." He hesitated before he added, "And they dance after goals, which is pretty cool too."

Coach Cleary's face was getting redder and redder, but before he could respond, Lucas McGoish got to his feet. Ben tensed up, ready for Lucas to throw out one of his nasty remarks, but instead he said, "I noticed that too. They're a lot cooler than I thought they'd be. One kid even complimented me on a pass I made."

"Same with me," Matty said.

Billy Clay nodded. "Did you see the backflip that kid did after scoring? That was pretty sweet."

All the boys started chattering, until they were silenced by the coach's whistle. "That's ENOUGH!" he hollered. "They're not your friends! They're just acting nice so you won't notice when they carve you up into a million little pieces! Now get out there and show NO MERCY!"

The referee blew his whistle, and as the team gathered on the field, Lucas told everyone to circle up.

"Don't listen to Coach," Lucas said. "Listen to Ben. Everyone relax, and let's have fun out there."

The team roared as one, "LET'S DO THIS!"

Ben felt something new in his chest.

It was team pride.

sees Lucas streaking down the left side, feeds him the ball . . .

Lucas crosses the ball into the middle, where Andre Hollins rises up

to get a head on it . . .

and it's in the net! It's a goal!!! West Harbor cuts the lead to 2–1!

2 1

As soon as the ball went in the net, the West Harbor players looked at each other, not sure what to do. Could they celebrate? *Should* they celebrate?

Ben answered that question by letting out a deafening "YYOOWWWSA!" and jumping on Andre's back. Two seconds later there was a giant pile of hugging, screaming kids.

"GUYS!" hollered Coach Cleary. "LET'S GET

FOCUSED! WE'RE STILL BEHIND!" But he was smiling. His voice was different.

Everything felt different.

The Jogo Bonito team regrouped, going into a circle of their own. They may have been nice guys, but they wanted to win just as badly as West Harbor.

The referee blew his whistle to get both teams ready for the restart.

"Let's go boys," said the ref. "Twenty minutes left."

This has been one of the best halves of soccer I've ever seen . . . both teams going at it, end-to-end action, playing great soccer. But no one has managed to put one in the net, so the score remains 2–1 in favor of Jogo Bonito . . .

As the time wound down, the game got more and more exciting, and the crowd was totally into it. So into it, in fact, that Ben's parents forgot that Ellie was holding a sixty-five-pound dog on a leash.

So when, with seven minutes left to play in the game, a squirrel decided to run across the field, a bunch of things happened, all within thirty seconds:

Lola saw the squirrel and lunged forward.

Ellie dropped the leash.

Lola charged onto the field, sprinting toward the squirrel.

The squirrel panicked and climbed up one of the goalposts, right next to Billy Clay.

Billy Clay, who had never been particularly fond of rodents of any kind, also panicked, and started running around in a circle yelling, "HELP, THERE'S A SQUIRREL! HELP, THERE'S A SQUIRREL!"

The coaches started yelling.

The parents started hollering.

The players started laughing.

And not just laughing.

LAUGHING.

Howling, screaming, cracking up, doubling over.

What is going on out there, folks?! I've seen a lot of wild things in my day, but I don't think I've ever seen a dog chase a squirrel up a goalpost in the middle of a championship game before! The game is stopped because . . . well, because all the players are too busy laughing to actually play soccer! Actually, I take that back . . . there is some soccer still being played by the dog! That's right, people, the dog now has the ball, and she's dribbling with her nose—quite well, in fact—a bunch of players are chasing her, but she's playing keep-away . . .

By the time the squirrel finally escaped, and a Jogo Bonito player grabbed Lola, and Billy Clay stopped hyperventilating, the kids were falling down in hysterics.

Diego, the goal scorer from Jogo Bonito, was laughing so hard Ben was afraid he was going to crack a few ribs.

Andre Hollins giggled until he started hiccuping uncontrollably. And Lucas McGoish was snorting like a small pig.

The whole field was filled with chortling, chuckling, and guffawing. And do you know what they say about laughter?

It's contagious.

Sure enough, the next thing you knew, EVERYONE was laughing. The parents, the referees, even Coach Cleary.

Finally, after Lola was satisfied that the squirrel was not catchable (this time!) and trotted back to her family, everyone was ready to continue the game.

"That was BONKERS!" Diego said to Ben. "Your dog is BONKERS!"

"Not bonkers," Ben told him. "She just likes squirrels."

"LIKES SQUIRRELS!" Diego started howling all over again. "LIKES SQUIRRELS! That's for sure!"

Coach Cleary gathered the team around and looked like he was about to make another one of his speeches, but then decided not to. Instead, he just shrugged, laughed a little, and said, "Go out there and have fun, boys."

Fun.

Now that was a game plan Ben could get behind.

The ball slides through to Ben, who is wide open . . . he lines up to shoot, the Jogo Bonito goalie comes out . . . Ben winds up to take a shot . . .

After the ball went in the net, everything exploded.

The whole team jumped on Lucas, screaming, but he pointed at Ben. "IT WAS ALL CLEATUS!" he yelled. "BEST PASS EVER!"

"Nice dummy," Ben said to Matty.

"Can't remember where I learned that," Matty said, smiling.

The crowd was going nuts. Coach Cleary was going nutsier. And then Lucas, whose eyes were still a tiny bit black and blue from his injury, suddenly went into a Flying Man dance of his own. Out went the arms, flapping back and forth, as he careened all over the field, squawking like a happy bird. All his teammates followed, and the next thing you knew there was a sea of Flying Men, just like in the Pizza League game against the Buffalo Chickens.

Ben couldn't believe it. So much had happened since then, but here he was, with a bunch of kids on a soccer field, having the time of his life.

Eventually the game continued, but it ended in a 2–2 tie, and West Harbor Academy and Jogo Bonito were declared co-champions.

After all the players from both teams congratulated each other, and Diego promised Ben he'd teach him how to do the double flip celebration, Lucas and Ben walked off the field together.

"That was the best game I've ever been a part of," Lucas said.

Ben looked surprised. "I thought you hated ties!"

Lucas thought about that for a second.

"Yeah, I thought I did too," he said. "I guess I've changed."

CHAPTER EIGHTEEN
THE ULTIMATE GOAL

After the game, Ben hugged his family, kissed his dog, and then found Jay-Jay and Annabella.

"You said if we won we'd go out for ice cream, and if we lost, you'd never speak to me again," he told Annabella. "But you didn't say what you'd do if we tied."

Her eyes were twinkling. "Let's go out for ice cream and I'll think about if I ever want to speak to you again."

Scooper Dooper was crowded, so everyone ordered their cones and shakes and sundaes and went outside to sit at a picnic table. For the first minute or so, no one said anything as they dove into their treats. Ben decided his caramel sundae was particularly delicious that day.

Then Jay-Jay pointed and said, "Hey, Ben, isn't that your coach?"

Ben looked up. Sure enough, Coach Cleary was walking toward them. Ben had a sudden jolt of uncertainty, wondering if the coach would still be mad about what he'd said at halftime.

"Uh-oh," he said, quietly.

But Annabella heard him, and said, "Uh-oh, what? You have nothing to be worried about, Benji."

Benji?

Ben wasn't sure how he felt about that nickname, but it was better than Cleatus.

"Hey, Ben, hi, everyone," said Coach Cleary as he approached their table. "Nothing better than ice cream after a hard-fought game, right?" Then he looked at Ben. "Got a sec?"

"Sure, Coach," Ben said. He glanced over at his parents and friends, who were all pretending not to pay attention.

"So, uh, Ben," Coach said. "I just wanted to . . . well, I just wanted to tell you what a good game you played and what a good season you had."

Ben stopped midbite. "Uh . . . really?"

"Really. You came a long way and learned a lot. As did some other people. And I'm not just talking about the kids." Coach was speaking softly, and Ben thought he sounded a bit nervous. "You seem to have a good handle on what the ultimate goal is when you're playing sports. And I admire that."

Ben was a little shocked, and it took him a few seconds to recover. But finally, he managed to say, "Thanks for saying that, Coach. I really appreciate it."

Coach Cleary said a few words to Ben's parents, then

he bent down and scratched Lola's ear. "I'm looking for someone with moves like yours," he told her. "If you want to play some soccer next season, give me a call."

Lola just looked up at him, disappointed that he didn't have any treats.

After Coach Cleary walked away, no one said anything for a minute. Then Ben's mom said, "Hey, Ben, can I ask you something?"

"Sure, Mom, what's up?"

She was looking at her son very intently. "Did you have a good time today?"

Ben rolled his eyes. "Of course, Mom. I mean, you saw it, right? Lola charged onto the field and a squirrel ran right over Billy Clay's face! It was awesome!"

"I'm not sure that's what Mom meant," Ben's dad said. "I think she meant, did you like playing in the game?"

Ben glanced over at Annabella and Jay-Jay, who were polishing off the last of their milkshakes. He winked at Ellie, who was looking sadly at her empty bowl. He petted Lola, who was waiting for some melted ice cream to hit the ground.

And then, finally, he looked at his parents.

"I did," Ben said. "I think I might even have loved it."

Jay-Jay and Annabella smiled while Ben hugged his parents.

"I love soccer too," announced Ellie. "Especially the home runs."

WHAT'S YOUR NICKNAME?

One of the most famous soccer players who ever lived was a Brazilian man named Edson Arantes do Nascimento, who was known by his nickname, Pelé, when he played. The whole world mourned when he passed away in 2022.

No one really knows how he got his nickname, or what it means. But that led to a lot of soccer stars becoming known by a single name or a nickname, including Chicharito, Baby Horse, Ronaldo, Kaká, or Neymar.

But what about you?

If you were a soccer star, what would your nickname be?

Probably not Cleatus, right?

Here are a few suggestions:

Pineapple

Lightning

Arnold

Kwikster

French Fry

Bizzy

Moodle

Can you come up with some nicknames?
They can be made-up words!

_____

_____

_____

_____

_____

_____

_____

_____

_____

POP QUIZ!

Ben's sister, Ellie, is not exactly an expert when it comes to soccer. But there are a lot of sports out there, and sometimes knowing all the rules can be confusing. Here's a quick quiz for you to see how much YOU know about sports, and how you keep score. You'll know some right off the bat, of course, but some others . . . well, give it a try!

DRAW STRAIGHT LINES MATCHING THE SPORT TO THE WAY YOU KEEP SCORE!

Baseball	Touchés
Football	Strokes
Soccer	Time
Basketball	Goals
Golf	Runs
Running	Touchdowns
Fencing	Points

ANSWER KEY:

baseball–runs
football–touchdowns
soccer–goals
basketball–points
golf–strokes
running–time
fencing–touchés

WHAT IS *YOUR* ULTIMATE GOAL?

It's important to do what you love.

And it's just as important to love what you do.

Out there in the big wide world, everyone loves to do different things. Maybe it's playing a sport, or maybe it's playing an instrument, or dancing, or learning a foreign language, or studying lizards.

Different people love to do different things, which is exactly how it should be!

What are the things YOU love to do? And why do you do them?

Think about it for a minute.

Do you do them because you want to win? Is it because you want to be good at what you do, or maybe even be the best? Is it because you want to enjoy it and have fun?

Or maybe it's a combination of all those things?

Write down your favorite things to do, and what your ultimate goal is in doing those things. And remember— there are no wrong answers. Just ask Ben Cutler, or Anna- bella Donatello, or even Lola—as long as you are doing what you love to do, and you love doing it, then you're all SET!

_____

_____

_____

_____

_____

_____

_____

_____

ACKNOWLEDGMENTS

Fun fact: In Erica Finkel's eighth-grade yearbook, under *Career Goals*, she wrote, "What I really want to do is edit a lot of sports books, because I love sports so very much!"

Okay, that might not be true, but here she is, editing my fourth book about kids and sports—and I just have to say, she is certainly cut out for the job. Erica is doing amazing work, and I thank her.

Thanks to Amy Thrall Flynn, who cares so deeply and so smartly.

I also want to thank Chelsea Hunter, Megan Carlson, Maggie Moore, Deena Micah Fleming, Emily Daluga, Maggie Lehrman, Andrew Smith, Jody Mosley, Kim Lauber, Hallie Patterson, Trish McNamara O'Neill, and everyone at Abrams who continues to support these books so beautifully.

Thanks so much to Lesley Vamos—this story has been made complete with her beautiful drawings.

And finally, thanks to the young athletes out there on all the fields, courts, and dirty patches of grass, whose joyous love of play is something we all need to remember, protect, and learn from.

THE WORM

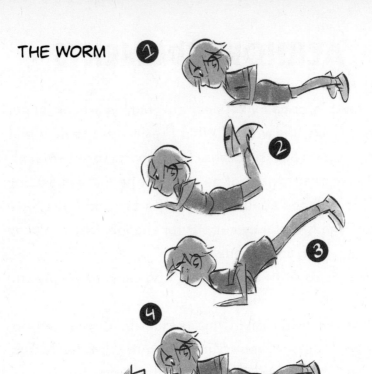

THE MOONDANCE

THE FLYING MAN DANCE

READ ON FOR A LOOK AT
THE NEXT INSTALLMENT OF
THE GOOD SPORTS LEAGUE!

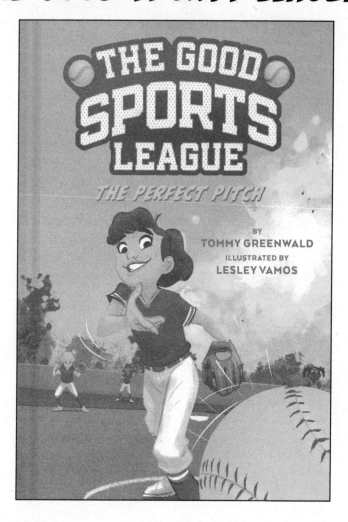

PROLOGUE

During the softball season, Annabella Donatello and her manager, Coach Grandy, had developed a routine.

Before the first inning of every game Annabella pitched, they would stand next to each other just outside the dugout, and Coach Grandy would look Annabella in the eye.

"Perfect day, perfect game, perfect pitch," the coach would say. Then she would hold out the ball. "Now go out there and get 'em."

Annabella would take the ball and say, "Perfectly happy to do so!"

This routine was their good luck charm, and one thing was for sure—it was definitely working.

Annabella Donatello had become the best pitcher in the league.

CHAPTER ONE
THE EVERYTHING GIRL

Annabella Donatello's mom sometimes called her daughter the "Everything Girl," because Annabella liked to do everything.

She liked to draw, she liked flying kites, she liked playing soccer for the Green Peppers in the Pizza League, she liked cooking, and she liked eating what she cooked.

She even liked doing math.

MATH?!?!

One day Annabella was watching television, and she saw a person juggling oranges.

"I want to try that," Annabella said.

"Please don't," her mom said. "It takes weeks to learn how to juggle, and in the meantime, I'll be scraping oranges off the wall."

Annabella learned how to juggle in four days, two hours, and forty-seven minutes, and no smushed oranges had to be scraped off any walls, which was a good thing, because Ms. Donatello was already a single mom who worked two jobs.

One of her jobs was the adoption coordinator at the West Harbor Animal Rescue Center. Annabella volunteered there whenever she could, because she loved dogs. Her favorite was Scruffy, an older mixed breed who came to the shelter missing one eye and half her hair. Scruffy was very sweet and playful but had yet to be adopted. Annabella loved playing with Scruffy.

She loved the cage-cleaning part less.

THE
FUN
PART

THE
NOT-SO-
FUN
PART

But of all the activities Annabella Donatello enjoyed, there were two that she loved most of all.

The first was softball.

Annabella started playing softball as soon as she could walk. She was a dominant pitcher, a superb fielder, and could hit the ball all the way to the next town.

The second thing Annabella loved more than anything was performing. She always seemed to be onstage: putting on plays for her mom, singing in the shower, telling stories at lunch.

"Do you think I could make it to Broadway one day?" she asked the school music teacher, Mr. Ketchnik.

Mr. Ketchnik thought for a moment, then said, "I think your passion and energy can take you as far as you want to go."

"Thanks!" said Annabella, before adding, "I think."

When Annabella was able to combine her two favorite things—softball and performing—it was the best thing of all!

So it was no wonder that after the big win against the Portsmouth Seasiders, when the team did their postgame chant, Annabella could be heard above everyone else.

We're the Bashers!

We're the Slashers!

We're the Mashers!

But mostly . . . we're the Smashers!

Goooooooooo SMASHERS!

Sadie Lederman, who was so serious about softball that she wore eye black under her eyes even when it wasn't sunny, glared at Annabella. "Do you always have to sing so loud?"

"YEEESSS!" sang Annabella, in her loudest voice.

Coach Grandy clapped her hands together. "Solid win out there today, girls. You fought really hard. But to be honest, the hitting wasn't great. In fact, it was the opposite of great. So even though we have a game tomorrow afternoon, we're going to have an extra batting practice in the morning at ten a.m."

All the girls nodded, except for one.

Annabella.

Instead, she raised her hand. "Excuse me, Coach? As much as I would love to go to this last-minute-unscheduled-not-on-the-calendar practice, I have my friend Jay-Jay's birthday party."

"Hey, wait a second," said Sadie. "I'm going to the party too, but it's not till eleven."

Annabella glared at Sadie. "Right, the party is at eleven, but Trini and I have to go to the mall to buy Jay-Jay's present first."

"Why do you always wait until the last minute?" Sadie asked.

"Why do you never mind your own business?" Annabella asked in return.

"You two, hush!" said Coach Grandy. "So, Annabella, you're saying you are unable to attend this practice?"

Annabella shook her head. "I'm sorry, I promised Trini," she said.

The coach did not look happy. "Yes, well speaking of promises, you also promised your full commitment to this program and this team, did you not?"

Annabella's ears started to burn. "I swear I'll be at pre-game warmups right on time!"

"Well, aren't we all so grateful for that," said Coach Grandy, with a sarcastic edge to her voice. As soon as she turned to gather up the equipment, Sadie wrinkled her nose at Annabella.

Annabella almost wrinkled her nose back but then decided not to.

She stuck out her tongue instead.

CHAPTER TWO

QUESTION: IS CAKE GOOD FOR YOU?

"How the heck did he do that?!?" Trini Tellez asked Annabella. Their eyes were as wide as the Grand Canyon.

"I have no idea," said Annabella. "And where's Jay-Jay?"

All the kids started murmuring as they realized Jay-Jay was nowhere to be found. Suddenly, Ben Cutler pointed up at a tree and cried out, "WHOA, NO WAY!" There was Jay-Jay, waving down at his friends.

"Here I am!" he shouted, excitedly.

The crowd is going **BONKERS**

ABOUT THE AUTHOR

TOMMY GREENWALD is the author of *Game Changer*, *Rivals*, and *Dinged*. *Game Changer* is on nineteen state lists, was an Amazon Best Book of the Month, a YALSA Top Ten Quick Pick for Reluctant Young Adult Readers, and a Junior Library Guild Premier selection. *Rivals* was also an Amazon Best Book of the Month, a Junior Library Guild selection, and a YALSA Quick Pick for Reluctant Young Adult Readers. Greenwald is also the author of the Crimebiters! and Charlie Joe Jackson series, among many other books for children. To read woefully outdated information about him, visit tommygreenwald.com.

ABOUT THE ILLUSTRATOR

LESLEY VAMOS earned a Bachelor's in digital media with high distinction from the University of New South Wales School of Art & Design, along with an honorary award in hand-drawn animation despite continuing to hold her pencil incorrectly. Lesley has been running her illustration and design business for over a decade and is passionate about telling stories that put good into the world. She lives in Sydney, Australia, with her partner, two littles, and small floofer, Penny.